W9-CFQ-387

SANTA WHO?

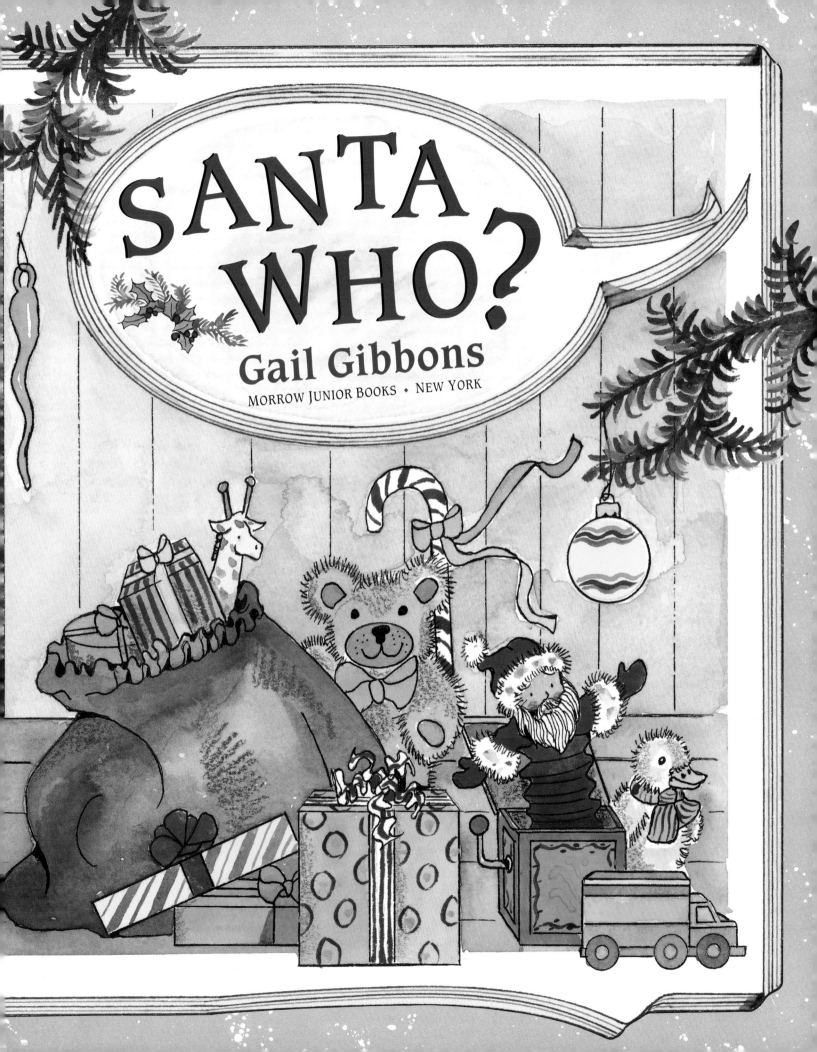

SANTA WHO?

Gail Gibbons

MORROW JUNIOR BOOKS • NEW YORK

**For my brother's family:
Ariana, Lisa, and
Guy Ortmann**

Watercolor, colored pencil, and black pen were used for the full-color
illustrations. The text type is 14-point Caxton Roman Bold.

Copyright © 1999 by Gail Gibbons

Published by Morrow Junior Books
a division of William Morrow and Company, Inc.
1350 Avenue of the Americas, New York, NY 10019
www.williammorrow.com

Printed in Hong Kong by South China Printing Company (1988) Ltd.

10 9 8 7 6 5 4 3 2

Library of Congress Cataloging-in-Publication Data
Gibbons, Gail.
Santa who? / Gail Gibbons.
p. cm.
Summary: Describes the origins and evolution of Santa Claus, from
the Turkish Saint Nicholas to the jolly, red-suited Santa of today.
Also discusses similar legendary figures in other cultures.
ISBN 0-688-15528-6 (trade) — ISBN 0-688-15529-4 (library)
1. Santa Claus—Juvenile literature.   [1. Santa Claus.]   I. Title.
GT4992.G5 1999   394.2663—dc21   98-48749   CIP AC

Santa Claus! He looks so kind and jolly. But the legend of this famous gift-giver began long ago, hundreds and hundreds of years before people thought of him as a round man dressed in a fur-trimmed suit.

According to the Bible, the first Christmas gifts were given about two thousand years ago, when three wise men saw a star shining brightly in the eastern sky. They believed it was a sign that a special child had been born.

The wise men followed the star until it came to rest over a stable in the city of Bethlehem. There they offered the baby Jesus gifts of gold and sweet-smelling frankincense and myrrh—gold for a great king, frankincense for a holy man, and myrrh for a miraculous healer. Jesus came to be called the Christ child from *Christos,* a Greek word that means "anointed," or "savior."

The original Santa Claus is thought to have been Saint Nicholas, who lived about seventeen hundred years ago. He was the Catholic bishop of Myra in the land now called Turkey, and he was known for his love of children and for his secret gifts to the poor.

Over time, many stories were told about this great man.
Some believed that he flew through the skies, looking for people
who needed his help. When surprise gifts were given at celebrations
and festivals, people began to say that they were really from Nicholas.

After he died on December 6 in the year 343, many people began to think of Nicholas as their special protector. Later the Greek Orthodox Church made him a saint. December 6 became a special gift-giving holiday called the Feast of Saint Nicholas. Nicholas was pictured riding a white horse, bearing gifts, and holding a sturdy crook in his hand. He was dressed in his bishop's clothes, a long red cape falling from his shoulders.

In one story about Saint Nicholas, a man had three daughters and no money to provide each a dowry, the gift a bride's family presents to the bride and groom when they marry. This was a terrible misfortune! But then Saint Nicholas, the secret gift-giver, dropped three bags of gold down their chimney. Soon all three daughters were happily married, and the legend began that gifts found on Saint Nicholas Day had come down the chimney.

As time passed, the spirit of Saint Nicholas the gift-giver took on many forms. The Dutch word for saint is *sinter,* and the shortened name for Nicholas is Cleas. In Holland, children called the saint Sinter Cleas. On the eve of December 6, they would place their shoes or stockings by the fireplace, along with carrots, sugar, or hay for Saint Nicholas's donkey. The next morning the offerings would be gone and gifts would be left in their place.

About five centuries ago, some religious leaders declared that it was wrong to worship saints or celebrate their holidays. For them, December 6 was not a proper day for gift giving. Not everyone agreed, but that's when some people began exchanging gifts on Christmas, a name that comes from the Old English Chistes Maesse, or "Christ's Mass." Since the Bible doesn't give a birth date for Jesus, early religious leaders had chosen December 25. That was around the time of the winter solstice, when festivals were held to mark the passing of winter and the coming of longer days and shorter nights. The festivals changed into the celebration of Jesus' birthday.

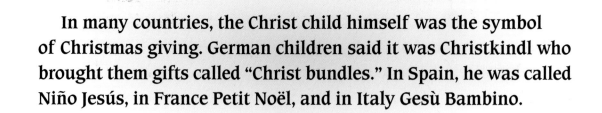

In many countries, the Christ child himself was the symbol of Christmas giving. German children said it was Christkindl who brought them gifts called "Christ bundles." In Spain, he was called Niño Jesús, in France Petit Noël, and in Italy Gesù Bambino.

In England, children received gifts from Father Christmas. The origins of this stern figure date to ancient Rome, where a Roman god named Saturn was said to watch over the winter festivals. The Romans brought him to England long ago, when it was part of the Roman Empire. As the winter festivals became celebrations of the birth of Christ, the image of Saturn slowly changed into that of Father Christmas.

In Northern Europe, little elves with long white whiskers were believed to be gift-givers. In Sweden, they were called Jule-tomar. In Denmark and Norway, they were called Jule-Nisser. On Christmas Eve, children put out bowls of rice pudding for the elves. Gifts always appeared by morning.

In Italy, there are many stories about an old woman named Befana, who gave gifts at Christmas. In one, she got lost bringing gifts to the Christ child. Every year after that, she left gifts for other children, hoping she might find the Christ child at last. In Russia, children believed that another old woman called Babushka left gifts because she felt so guilty for steering the wise men in the wrong direction on their trip to Bethlehem.

In 1624, the Dutch sent a fleet of ships to the New World of the Americas. The Dutch established a colony called New Amsterdam, and with them they brought their belief in Sinter Cleas.

England captured the Dutch city in 1664 and renamed it New York. The English children found Sinter Cleas far more appealing than Father Christmas. So they began the custom of celebrating Christmas with a gift-giver who looked more and more like Sinter Cleas.

In 1809, Washington Irving, the famous author of "The Legend of Sleepy Hollow," published a humorous book called *Knickerbocker's History of New York*. His description of the way the Dutch celebrated Saint Nicholas Day was particularly festive. He wrote of stockings hung at the chimney being miraculously filled by the good Saint Nicholas, the great giver of gifts, especially to children.

Washington Irving pictured Saint Nicholas as a pipe-smoking man who loved fun and rode across rooftops in a horse-drawn wagon piled with gifts. His book was read by many people, and it influenced their image of Saint Nicholas.

One man who read Washington Irving's book was Clement Clarke Moore. On Christmas Eve, 1822, he was leaving to buy the Christmas turkey when his children begged, "Bring us a Christmas surprise." As his sleigh streaked through the snowy streets, he had a wonderful idea. He would fulfill his children's wish with a poem about Saint Nicholas.

That night Clement Clarke Moore gathered his children around and began reciting, "'Twas the night before Christmas, when all through the house, not a creature was stirring, not even a mouse."

A Dutch handyman who worked for the Moore family was the inspiration for Saint Nicholas. When the saint appeared in the poem, he was described as "dressed all in fur, from his head to his foot," and as "chubby and plump, a right jolly old elf." Earlier pictures had shown Saint Nicholas with only one reindeer. Clement Clarke Moore gave him eight: "Now, Dasher! Now, Dancer! Now, Prancer and Vixen! On, Comet! On, Cupid! On, Donder and Blitzen!"

The poem, called "An Account of a Visit from St. Nicholas," was printed in a newspaper in 1823. In 1848, it was published as the text in an illustrated book. Many other versions followed, and by 1860 Clement Clarke Moore's Christmas surprise was one of the most famous poems ever written.

More and more people were celebrating the merriment of Christmas. Because of this, between 1836 and 1890, December 25 became a legal holiday in all the United States and its territories. And the old Dutch name Sinter Cleas became Santa Claus.

No one added more to the image of Santa Claus than a cartoonist named Thomas Nast. In 1863, he drew a picture of Santa Claus for *Harper's Weekly* magazine. Each year he drew Santa again, changing the details little by little.

In 1886, Nast's image of Santa Claus had become that of the round, jolly man whom we're so familiar with today.

Thomas Nast was also the first illustrator to draw Santa in his workshop at the North Pole, where he was shown answering stacks of letters from children.

As time went by, more and more characters joined in the Santa Claus legend. Elves are shown helping Santa make toys, and there is often a Mrs. Claus, who is just as plump and jolly as her husband.

At Christmastime, Santa's everywhere! He stands on street corners, ringing bells to collect money for the needy. He's found in stores and malls, listening as children read their Christmas lists. He appears on Christmas cards, in movies, on wrapping paper, and in songs.

Over the years, many cultures have added to our image of
Santa Claus. What a jolly and joyous gift-giver he has become!